Jasper John Dooley
Public ᵛ Enemy #1
Library

Jasper John Dooley

Public Library Enemy #1

Written by Caroline Adderson
Illustrated by Mike Shiell

Kids Can Press

For Yasemin and Sheila, Book Heroes — C.A.

Text © 2016 Caroline Adderson
Illustrations © 2016 Kids Can Press

This is a work of fiction and any resemblance of characters to persons living or dead is purely coincidental.

Kids Can Press acknowledges the financial support of the Government of Ontario, through the Ontario Media Development Corporation's Ontario Book Initiative; the Ontario Arts Council; the Canada Council for the Arts; and the Government of Canada, through the CBF, for our publishing activity.

Published in Canada by
Kids Can Press Ltd.
25 Dockside Drive
Toronto, ON M5A 0B5

Published in the U.S. by
Kids Can Press Ltd.
2250 Military Road
Tonawanda, NY 14150

www.kidscanpress.com

Edited by Yasemin Uçar
Series designed by Rachel Di Salle
Designed by Julia Naimska
Illustrations by Mike Shiell, based on illustrations by Ben Clanton in Jasper John Dooley, Books 1–4

This book is smyth sewn casebound.
Manufactured in Shen Zhen, Guang Dong, P.R. China, in 10/2015 by Printplus Limited

CM 16 0 9 8 7 6 5 4 3 2 1

Library and Archives Canada Cataloguing in Publication

Adderson, Caroline, author
    Public library enemy #1 / written by Caroline Adderson ; illustrated by Mike Shiell.

(Jasper John Dooley ; 6)
ISBN 978-1-77138-015-7 (bound)

    I. Shiell, Mike, illustrator II. Title. III. Title: Jasper John Dooley, public library enemy #1.
IV. Series: Adderson, Caroline. Jasper John Dooley ; 6.

PS8551.D3267P832016   jC813'.54   C2015-904305-0

Kids Can Press is a ſℓᎾ∩ᒍᔆ™ Entertainment company

Contents

Chapter 1

After school, Jasper John Dooley and his friend Ori
rode their bikes to the library with Jasper's mom.
Mom needed to pick up something from the store.
"I'll be back in ten minutes," she said. "Stay in the
children's area, okay?"

"Okay!"

Jasper and Ori raced each other up the steps. They
got to the top at the same time and found a sign
taped to the door.

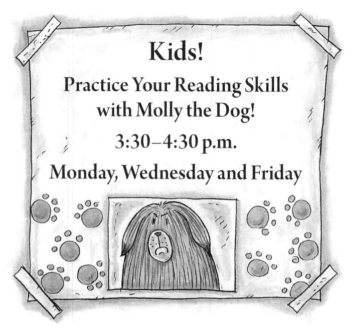

Kids!

Practice Your Reading Skills with Molly the Dog!

3:30–4:30 p.m.

Monday, Wednesday and Friday

Under the words was a picture of a very grumpy dog.

Ori said, "I don't think I've ever seen a dog frown before."

"What day is it?" Jasper asked.

"Monday," Ori said.

"What time?"

They burst into the library and looked around for the clock. It was high on the wall, above the desk where the librarian sat like a hen on a nest. Jasper didn't like time with hands. He liked time with just numbers.

"Is it three thirty?" he asked the librarian.

She looked at the clock. "It's a little past four." She smiled at Jasper and Ori and pointed to the long, long line behind them. It snaked from the children's area almost to the computers. So so so many kids wanted to read to Molly the Dog!

"Are we too late?" Ori asked.

"Everybody reads for five minutes," the librarian told them. "Unless some readers get tired of waiting, you'll have a better chance on Wednesday."

"So some kids might get tired of waiting?" Jasper asked.

"I suppose they might," the librarian said.

"Let's get in line," Jasper told Ori.

First, they needed to see Molly the Dog up close. They peeked around the shelves into the children's area. Zoë from their class was sitting in the big, comfy chair with the flower splotches. There was a pile of hair beside her.

"Is that Molly?" Ori asked.

The two of them crept closer to get a better look. When they were almost beside Zoë, Jasper recognized the book in her hands. It was the ballerina book Ms. Tosh had started reading aloud at school, the one about Cheeky the Squirrel.

"Cheeky, Cheeky, Cheeky," Zoë droned on.

The pile of hair beside Zoë looked like a wig that had blown off somebody's head, until the wig lifted

its funny pushed-in face and stared straight at Jasper
with its huge brown eyes. Her tail wagged, but her face
was still frowning. She didn't like that book at all!

Jasper reached out to pat Molly. Then Ori did.
Finally, Zoë noticed the boys crouched beside her.
"Jasper John Dooley! Ori Spivak! Wait your turn!"

Jasper and Ori scurried back around the bookshelf.

"Molly hates Zoë's book," Jasper told Ori. "It's about ballerinas. She probably doesn't even know what a ballerina is."

"The thing is, we need a dog book, not a ballerina book."

"Or a book about things dogs like."

"What do dogs like?" Ori asked.

They went back to the librarian.

"It really doesn't matter what you read," the librarian told them. "She just enjoys sitting on your lap and listening to the sound of your voice."

Jasper found that hard to believe. It was probably listening to boring books from three thirty to four thirty Monday, Wednesday and Friday that made

Molly so grumpy. Jasper felt grumpy, too, whenever Ms. Tosh read them books about ballerinas.

"What kind of dog is Molly?" Ori asked.

"Pekingese, I believe," the librarian said. "But I'm not one-hundred-percent sure. I'm a Cat Person."

Ori asked where the dog books were. The librarian got up and led them over to the shelf.

There weren't any books about Pekingese dogs.

"What about this?" Ori asked Jasper, holding out a book about Saint Bernards. "Or this?" He showed him one about Labrador retrievers.

"Let's find something else," Jasper said. "But no ballerinas."

"No ballerinas," Ori agreed. He moved to the next shelf and pulled down a book about rockets. "She'll love this!"

"How do you know she'll love it?" Jasper asked, but Ori had already opened the book and started reading.

Jasper glanced over his shoulder. Zoë had finished her turn, and now a boy with glasses was reading to Molly in the big flower-splotch chair. On the cover of his book was a picture of a bulldozer. Molly was frowning her head off.

Jasper started pulling down books, looking for something — anything — that Molly would enjoy. Then Mom showed up.

"They have a new reading program," she said.

"We know," Jasper told her. "We're looking for a book that will make Molly stop frowning. It can't be about ballerinas or bulldozers."

"You'll have to pick it for next time," Mom said.

"There's still a chance we'll get to read to Molly," Jasper told her.

Mom pointed to the line. Eight fidgety kids were still waiting. Then Mom showed Jasper her watch. All he saw was hands.

"There are only ten minutes left," she told him.

"Some of those kids might give up and go home," Jasper said.

Mom sighed. "Sorry, but that's what *we* have to do, Jasper."

"But we didn't get a turn!"

They went to check out the books. Mom had to steer Ori by the back of his neck because his face was in the rocket book. She had to drag Jasper because he didn't want to leave. She handed him his library card to slide across the counter to the librarian.

"Cheer up, Jasper J. Dooley," the librarian said. "Molly's here three days a week." She checked out Ori's book next and told him, "You come back, too, Ori D. Spivak."

They left the library, Mom and Jasper both a little grumpy.

Ori was reading so hard he didn't notice.

Chapter 2

The next day, Ms. Tosh read aloud again from the Cheeky the Squirrel book. As soon as Ms. Tosh said the word *ballet*, Jasper flopped onto his table. He put a finger on the stopper part of each ear and pressed it again and again. That way Ms. Tosh sounded like she was reading underwater.

"Glub-glub-glub. Glub-glub-glub."

Molly should have pushed her paws to her ears like this yesterday at the library when Zoë was reading to her. If Molly even had paws and ears.

Jasper hadn't noticed any under all her hair.

Then the recess bell rang. Luckily, Jasper heard it through the glubbing. He and Ori ran outside together. The girls raced past them and started playing one of their crazy games around the playground equipment. This time they were stuffing each other's socks with pinecones and twirling around with knobby ankles. Jasper and Ori climbed to the top of the jungle gym and sat there, swinging their legs. Jasper was still thinking about Molly.

"Didn't Molly look like a wig?" he asked Ori.

"That's what we should have read to her," Ori said. "A book about wigs."

Jasper laughed. "Let's go back today. Maybe they have a wig book."

Ori said, "Sure."

"Maybe we can find some wigs to wear!"

They laughed and laughed until Jasper remembered the poster that said Monday, Wednesday and Friday from three thirty to four thirty.

"Oh, it's Tuesday," he said, just before he got an idea.

After school, Mom was waiting to walk them home. "Can Ori come over?" Jasper asked.

"Sure," Mom said.

"Oh, good," Ori said. "We're going to practice our reading skills!"

Mom said, "Really? I've never seen you two so enthusiastic about schoolwork."

"We're enthusiastic," Jasper told her. "We're so so so enthusiastic!"

Ori ran down the alley to his house to let his mom know he had a playdate. Jasper and Mom waited. When Ori came back carrying the book about rockets, they walked on.

Jasper told Mom, "We need a big piece of paper."

"What for?" she asked.

"And we need small pieces of paper," Ori said.

"Why small pieces of paper?" Jasper asked.

"Tickets!" Ori said.

"What are you two up to?" Mom asked as she unlocked the door. "I'm really curious."

"It's a surprise," Jasper said.

"The paper's in the craft cupboard. I'll make you a snack while you work on your surprise."

Jasper took a piece of yellow construction paper from the craft cupboard and felt pens from the jar.

Ori found scrap paper and scissors. They went to Jasper's room.

Ori folded and refolded a piece of paper to make lines. He cut along the lines until he made thirty-two tickets. On each one he wrote a number.

"What if more than thirty-two pets come?" he asked.

"We'll make more tickets," Jasper said.

Jasper's sign read:

Jasper + Ori
will read to your Pets
(Books They will LIKE!!!)
3:30 - 4:30
Bring Your Dog or Cat or Hamster
Tusday and Thursday
and maybe other days too

Then they went into the kitchen for their snack, which was blueberries and cheese cubes. Jasper brought the sign.

"What a good idea," Mom said. "You can set up in the front yard, like a lemonade stand."

"The thing is," Ori told her, "that's what we're going to do."

"And it's nice of you to include cats and hamsters," Mom said.

"Some people are Cat People," Jasper said. "Some people are Dog People. Some people are Hamster People."

"What are you?" Mom asked.

"I'm a Molly the Dog Person," he said. "But only on Monday, Wednesday and Friday. I'm an All Pets Person the rest of the time."

Ori looked over the sign again. "What about Bird People?"

Jasper ran back to his room for the felt pen. He added *bird* to the sign.

Then he added *rabbit*. "We don't want to leave any kind of people out," he said.

"You'd better take the pen outside with you," Mom said.

"Good idea," Jasper said.

Jasper and Ori and Mom took two trips to carry out the other things they needed: their snack, Jasper's small table and two small chairs, the library books Jasper had borrowed yesterday, Ori's rocket book and an empty jam jar for the used tickets. They set the table and chairs right beside the sidewalk where everybody would pass. Ori found a rock to hold down the pile of tickets in case it got windy. Mom taped the sign to the tree.

"I hope you get a lot of customers," she said before she went back inside.

Jasper and Ori ate the blueberries and cheese cubes while they waited. After a few minutes, Jasper got up and added *guinea pig* to the sign. Ori started reading the book about rockets.

They waited.

"Here's something I could read to Molly," Ori told Jasper after a few minutes. "It's about a dog that went to space in a rocket."

Jasper pictured Molly in a rocket ship. In the picture she was frowning. "I really don't think Molly would like that."

Ori flipped the pages and read some more.

"We could go to space in a real rocket," he said. "We'd just need two hundred and fifty dollars with three zeros at the end."

"Two hundred and fifty dollars?" Jasper said. "That's a lot."

He got up and wrote *snake* on the sign.

"Please cross that out," Ori said.

Somebody was coming. Jasper dashed back to his chair. From the other end of the block, somebody was walking toward them holding a leash. At the end of the leash was an animal. A so so big animal.

"Is … Is that a horse?" Ori asked.

Jasper squinted. Yes! A woman was walking toward them leading a shaggy black and brown horse. Jasper jumped up and quickly added *horse* to the sign.

But as the horse got closer they saw it was Rollo, who only looked like a big shaggy horse with its ears hanging down. Rollo belonged to Isabel from their class. The woman walking Rollo was Isabel's nanny, Mandy. Whenever Mandy walked Rollo by the school at recess, all the kids rushed over to pat him.

As soon as Rollo saw Jasper and Ori, he bounded toward them, nearly pulling the leash out of Mandy's hand. Ori leaped up and ducked behind the tree so he wouldn't get clobbered by Rollo's big, waggy tail, or licked by Rollo's big, slobbery tongue. Jasper wasn't afraid. He patted Rollo.

Mandy read the sign on the tree. "Hey, Rollo. Let's stop and hear a story. Sit, boy."

Rollo sat on the grass. "He needs a ticket," Ori said. He crept out from behind the tree, lifted the rock and handed Mandy ticket Number 1. She put it in the empty jam jar.

Jasper held up the books for Rollo to choose. Rollo licked the one about rockets. He liked rockets. Or he liked the cheese-cube taste Ori's fingers had smeared on the book.

"Read to him about the dog who went to space," Ori said, scooting behind the tree again.

The dog who went to space was named Laika. She was the first dog astronaut in the world.

Rollo really liked the sound of Jasper's voice as he read. His big, waggy tail began slashing back and forth. Then Rollo flopped onto the ground and rolled over. He wriggled in the grass like his back was itchy.

"He's not even listening," Ori said.

Rollo had lost focus.

Jasper closed the book. "That's enough. Thanks, Rollo."

It was fun reading to Rollo, but not as much fun as reading to Molly would have been because Rollo couldn't sit in Jasper's lap. If he did, it would be Very Dangerous.

"Good reading," Mandy said. She reached in her pocket and took out some change. Jasper and Ori couldn't believe their eyes when she dropped it in the jar.

"Thanks!" they said.

After Rollo and Mandy left, Jasper and Ori dumped the change onto the table and divided it. "I didn't expect her to pay us," Jasper said.

"The thing is, neither did I!"

Ori started to count the money, but Jasper said, "Forget the math!" He swept half the coins into the jar. "I wonder who'll come by next? Another Dog Person? Or maybe a Hamster Person?"

"I wonder if they'll pay us," Ori said.

They waited a long time, but nobody else came by with a pet they could read to. Finally, Mom called out that it was four thirty. Ori helped Jasper bring everything inside. Then he went home with the book about rockets, across the alley and one house down.

Chapter 3

After supper, Mom had to go to a meeting. Jasper and Dad stayed home. Jasper brought a library book and the jar with Mandy's money to the living room, where Dad was watching golf on TV. The book was about toilet-paper-tube crafts. He stood in front of Dad and shook the jar so it jangled.

Dad looked up.

"You know how at a coffee shop they always have a jar next to the cash register?" Jasper asked. "How does it work?"

"If the server does a good job, you put your change in the jar. It's called a tip jar," Dad said.

"Isabel's nanny gave me a tip for reading to Rollo," Jasper said. "I didn't ask for money."

"You can't ask for a tip. You just do a good job and hope you'll get one."

"Oh," Jasper said.

He set the tip jar on the arm of the sofa. Then he pulled ticket Number 2 out of his pocket and handed it to Dad.

"What's this?" Dad asked.

"It's your ticket. You can put it in the tip jar, too."

Dad did, and Jasper settled down beside him and opened the book. "Wow!" he said. "Look at all the stuff you can make from toilet-paper tubes."

Baskets, bird feeders, pencil holders, mobiles,

penguins, sheep, spiders, dragons, race cars, binoculars, Christmas crackers, hanging lanterns, napkin rings …

"I could make a lint holder," Jasper said. "I could make you a golf-ball holder."

"Sorry," Dad said, looking from the TV to Jasper. "What did you say?"

"What do you want to learn how to make?" Jasper showed him the book.

"Whatever you want," Dad said.

"I got this book to practice my reading skills with Molly, the grumpy dog at the library," Jasper told Dad. "She's going to love this book when I go back to read it to her. She'll be happy it's not about ballerinas or bulldozers."

Jasper put a pillow in his lap. "The best way to

practice your reading skills is with a dog in your lap, but we don't have one, so I'm going to read to you and this pillow about how to make a spider out of a toilet-paper tube."

"Hold on," Dad said.

On the TV, a man in a pink shirt tapped the ball into a hole. "Yes!" Dad said. Then he turned to Jasper. "Okay. I'm listening."

"Materials," Jasper began.

He read the list of things you needed to make a spider out of a toilet-paper tube: scissors, glue, construction paper, pipe cleaners, felt pens, tape, string. When he had finished reading the list, he read the instructions. Then he looked at Dad.

Now Dad was watching a man in a yellow shirt tap the ball into a hole. He hadn't listened to a word Jasper had read. Jasper closed the book.

"Finished?" Dad asked. "Good job, Jasper."

"Really?" Jasper snatched up the tip jar and hoped. But instead of tipping Jasper for his reading, Dad told him it was time to get ready for bed.

Jasper shuffled off. The tip jar was no more jangly than it had been before he read to Dad.

In the bathroom, Jasper set the book about toilet-paper-tube crafts on the edge of the tub and turned on the water. He added a big squirt of bubble bath. Mom always read in the bath. It was her favorite place to read. Usually Jasper played or piled bubbles on his head and sculpted them into horns. But tonight he was more interested in toilet-paper tubes. He checked how much toilet paper was left on the roll — lots — then undressed and stepped into the tub. He lifted one leg over the side into the hot bubbly water, then the other, so so so carefully, so he wouldn't get the book wet.

Jasper sat down, but when he reached for the book, his hands were wet. If he read the book with wet hands, the pages would get wet and wavy. They might even stick together. If that happened, the library might make him pay for the book. It had happened once, the time Mom forgot her book outside on a lawn chair and it rained.

So so so carefully, Jasper stepped out of the tub to dry his hands on the towel. So so so carefully, he got back in, lifting one leg over the edge, then the other.

Bloop!

Jasper screamed.

Chapter 4

Dad burst into the bathroom. By then Jasper had scooped up the book and was standing in the tub holding it, both Jasper and the book dripping with water and bubble bath suds.

"I was so so so careful!" Jasper wailed.

"Don't worry, Jasper. It'll be fine," Dad said. "I know just what to do."

"What?"

"It's wet, isn't it? We just have to dry it. Finish your bath then put on your pajamas."

Dad hurried away with the dripping book.

Jasper dried himself off and dressed for bed. He found Dad in the kitchen staring through the oven window the way he'd stared at the TV. The book was lying open on the top rack.

"You're cooking it?" he asked Dad.

"I thought of putting it in the clothes dryer, but that would make things worse. Do you want some nachos? The oven's on."

Jasper said yes.

"Okay. You keep watch. Tell me if you smell smoke."

Dad poured tortilla chips into a pan. He took the cheese from the fridge and grated it. It fell like orange snow onto the chips.

"Don't watch me," Dad told Jasper. "Watch the book."

"Right!" Jasper turned back to the oven window.

After a minute, he thought of something. "Shouldn't we turn the pages? They might stick together."

Dad clapped his hand across his forehead. "Jasper John, you astound me! I didn't think of that. Open the oven."

Jasper pulled the door open, and Dad slid the pan of nachos in next to the book. Then he turned a page.

"Keep watching," he told Jasper on his way back to the living room.

Jasper watched. The pages already looked wavy. After a minute, he called, "The pages are getting wavier! And the cheese is melting!"

"Don't worry about the pages," Dad called back. "We'll iron them later!"

"The cheese is bubbling!" Jasper called. "And we need to turn the page!"

Dad came back and put on an oven mitt. Jasper opened the door for him to take out the nachos. The hand not wearing the big, clumsy oven mitt turned a page in the book.

"Looking good," he said. "We'll lower the temperature a bit. Can you get the salsa? And the sour cream?"

Jasper climbed onto an open bottom drawer so he could reach the bowls in the cupboard. He spooned out the salsa and the sour cream then carried the two bowls to the table. They sat down to eat the nachos.

The cheese stretched so so far off his chip trying to stay with the rest of the cheese. But it didn't unstick from the chip.

"Does cheese have glue in it?" Jasper asked.

Dad scooped some salsa onto his chip. "It doesn't,

but that's an interesting idea, Jasper. If there were cheese glue, you could glue different foods together before you eat them."

As they ate, they talked about the best foods to glue with cheese glue. Broken crackers could be glued back together.

"Or broken celery sticks", Dad said.

"Yuck," said Jasper. "You could glue down pepper. So you don't breathe it in by accident and —"

Jasper was going to say "sneeze," but just then a so so so so loud *BLEEEEEEEEEEEEEEP!!!!!!* interrupted him. He and Dad jumped right out of their chairs.

Thick black smoke was pouring from the oven.

"FIRE!!!" Dad and Jasper yelled.

Dad ran for the fire extinguisher in the cupboard.

Jasper kept on yelling, "FIRE!!! FIRE!!! FIRE!!!"
and the smoke alarm kept on shrieking
BLEEEEEEEEEEEEEEP!!!!!!

"Open the back door, Jasper! Open the window!"
BLEEEEEEEEEEEEEEP!!!!!!

Jasper raced to the door and flung it open. Dad
yanked out the pin on the fire extinguisher. He
crouched low with the extinguisher under his arm and
moved toward the oven like he was sneaking up on it.

"Be careful, Dad!" Jasper shouted over the
BLEEEEEEEEEEEEEEP!!!!!!

Dad pulled open the oven. More and more
smoke poured into the room. When the worst of it
had cleared, they could see the book. Flames were
gobbling up its pages.

"Dad, shoot!" Jasper yelled. "Shoot!"

Dad aimed the nozzle and fired. The book,
hidden by smoke a moment before, disappeared
again in the white spray of the fire extinguisher.
Jasper and Dad coughed and coughed.

BLEEEEEEEEEEEEEEP!!!!!!

When the spray cleared, Dad said, "Phew. That was a close one."

Jasper peered in at the book and cringed.

"We put out the fire, Dad. But I think we killed the book."

They opened all the doors and windows. They waved tea towels around. Finally, the alarm stopped. Dad found some air-freshener spray and sprayed it all around.

But the house still smelled of smoke when Mom got home.

"What burned?" she asked first thing.

"We made nachos," Dad said.

Jasper was already in bed, listening to Mom and

Dad talking in the hall. When Mom came into Jasper's room to say good night, she asked, "What did you and Dad do?"

"Nothing." Jasper pulled the covers up to his eyes.

"That sounds like fun."

Mom laughed. She kissed his forehead, then left him lying in the dark thinking about the "nothing" that had happened. How the book had blooped as it sank under the water. Jasper had thought he'd killed the book then, but he hadn't. It hadn't even died when it caught on fire. Not until Dad shot it. Then Dad flung it, all wavy and burned and covered in foam, out the back door.

Nobody would ever read that book again.

Chapter 5

At breakfast the next day, Jasper made himself a piece of toast while Dad made Jasper's lunch.

"Where's the book now?" Jasper asked.

"It's still in the backyard," Dad said. "We'll dispose of it on the way to school."

The toast popped and Jasper carried it to the table. "What do you mean, 'dispose of it'?"

"Get rid of it. We should hurry or you'll get the lates, Jasper."

Jasper buttered and jammed his toast. Usually, he

liked spreading the jam in stripes, using different kinds
of jam. Stripes kept the flavors separate. Today, though,
he picked just blueberry, gulped down his toast and
ran to get dressed. They left by the back door. Jasper
followed Dad, who was carrying an empty plastic bag.

The book was lying face down in the grass. It was
black with an ugly white crust sticking to it. When
they got closer, the stinky smell of it made Jasper yuck
and plug his nose.

"We're going to have to pay for it now," he said.

Jasper bent over the book and looked for a price. It was hard to read what was written there because the cover was so burned. Jasper got down on his hands and knees. He saw a two and a five and two zeros. He gagged and scrambled to his feet again.

Dad said, "They'll send us a bill at some point. Keep an eye on the mail. If you see something from the library, bring it to me. I'll take care of it."

"The time Mom left her book out on the lawn chair and it rained? She didn't wait for the bill. She took the book back to the library the next day and paid for it. I went with her."

"Jasper, it's one thing to show up with a book that got left out in the rain. It's another to show up with this." Dad picked up the book and held it in front of

Jasper's face. Jasper stepped back. The book looked so so so horrible and smelled so so so sour and burned!

"If the librarians saw that book, we'd have to tell them that we drowned it, then set it on fire, then shot it with the extinguisher."

"Exactly, Jasper."

"We're Book Killers," Jasper said.

Dad laughed, but Jasper didn't. He said, "Mom paid right away because she didn't feel good about using the library when she'd ruined a book. That's what she said."

"I wouldn't feel good about bringing this book into the library," Dad said. He dropped it in the plastic bag. The hand that had held the book was smeared with horrible black stuff. He wiped it on the grass.

Dad walked over to the garbage bin that stood beside the garage. He flipped open the lid and dropped the book in. Then they left for school.

"If we had brought the book back," Jasper said on the way, "do you think they would ever have let us in the library again?"

"I doubt it," Dad said. "Nobody likes a Book Killer."

After Calendar and Star of the Week, Ms. Tosh asked everybody to get together with their reading buddies. Jasper and Ori were reading buddies. They were reading buddies, friends and neighbors. They dove into the Book Nook together and stretched out on the cozy pillows. Ori had his library book about rockets with him.

"Look," Ori said. "It shows you how to make a rocket out of a soda bottle."

"You have to take good care of that book," Jasper told Ori. "You don't want anything bad to happen to it. If you accidentally drown it or set it on fire or shoot it, they might not let you back in the library to read to Molly."

"How could I drown it or set it on fire?" Ori asked.

"You could drop it in the bath, then put it in the oven."

"But how could I shoot it?" Ori asked. "I don't have a gun."

"You could use a fire extinguisher."

Ori threw back his head and laughed so hard that Jasper could see the dangly thing at the back of his throat wiggling around like a worm on a hook.

Ms. Tosh came over because Ori was laughing. They were supposed to be reading silently. "Where's your book, Jasper?" Ms. Tosh asked.

"Something happened to it," he said.

"What happened?" Ms. Tosh asked.

"I'd rather not say."

Ms. Tosh crossed her arms and gave him a look he had to obey.

He got up and pulled a book off the Book Nook shelf, sat back down and opened it. Only then did he notice it was one of those Cheeky the Squirrel books. Too late! Ms. Tosh was still standing over him with crossed arms.

He dragged his eyes over the page, but all he read was glub, glub, glub.

Chapter 6

After school, Mom got the lates. Jasper and Ori sat on the steps and talked while they waited for her to show up.

"Is twenty-five dollars a lot?" Jasper asked.

"It's a lot, but twenty-five with zeros is a lot lot more. A ride in a real rocket is twenty-five and four zeros. The more zeros after the number, the more it costs. My mom explained it to me. If you wanted to buy your own rocket, you couldn't because it has so many zeros."

"What about twenty-five with two zeros?" Jasper said.

Ori got up and found a stick. Under the trees there wasn't any grass, just dirt. He wrote 2-5-0-0. "That's a lot. A lot more than twenty-five dollars." Ori threw down the stick.

"It is?" Jasper said.

Mom appeared, waving and calling, "Sorry I'm late!" She stopped when she saw Jasper buckled over on the steps because of the two zeros. "What's wrong, Jasper?"

"I feel sick!" Jasper wailed.

"Too sick to visit Nan?" Mom asked.

Every Wednesday after school Jasper went to Nan's. He didn't want to miss his Wednesday visit. He unfolded himself and came down the steps of the school, clutching the handrail for support. "I'm okay now, I think."

First, Mom and Jasper walked Ori home. Ori talked on and on about how to build a rocket out of a soda bottle. Jasper didn't say anything but good-bye. Then he and Mom continued on to Nan's.

"Are you sure you're okay, Jasper? You're awfully

quiet. Did something happen at school today?"

"Zero happened at school," Jasper said.

"That's good because Nan is really looking forward to hearing you read to Molly."

"What?" Jasper cried.

Mom looked at her watch. "Maybe we should have ridden our bikes. But we might still be one of the first ones in line if we hurry. Nan's meeting us there. She'll listen to you read to Molly, then you'll go home with her."

"No library!" Jasper said, waving his arms.

"But Jasper, two days ago you were so excited about reading to Molly. What happened?" Mom asked.

Jasper did want to read to Molly, but now he owed the library for the book about toilet-paper-tube crafts that he'd killed. He owed a lot more than twenty-five dollars. They wouldn't blame Dad even though he had set the book on fire and shot it, and Jasper had only drowned it. The person they would blame was the person whose name was on the library card.

That person was Jasper J. Dooley.

Then Jasper thought of something. If he read to Nan, he'd probably get a tip. He needed tips — so so so many tips! — so he could pay for the book.

"Today is Wednesday," Jasper said. "Today I'm excited about reading to Nan."

Mom phoned Nan as they were walking. "Jasper says he doesn't want to go to the library after all. He insists on going straight to your place."

"Tell her I'm going to read to her," Jasper said.

"And he wants to read to you," Mom told Nan.

Nan met them in the jungley lobby. After they said good-bye to Mom, Nan let Jasper press the elevator buttons the way she always did. "I was looking forward to seeing that little dog," she told Jasper.

"Me, too!" Jasper said. He felt all watery inside, wondering if he'd ever get a chance to read to Molly.

Before Nan could ask why he didn't want to meet her at the library, the elevator doors opened. Jasper dashed in and made a horrible face in the mirrored wall. He and Nan always made horrible faces when they rode up to her apartment. They had contests to see who made the most horriblest face. Jasper always won except when Nan pushed her glasses frames into her eye sockets so her eyes stretched down.

Today Jasper's face was almost as horrible as that. Nan said, "Jasper! Stop! You're scaring me!"

"That's the face of a Book Killer," Jasper told her.

"It's horrible," Nan said.

"I know."

The elevator reached Nan's floor. Jasper pressed the button again. They went down and up three more times. When they finally stepped out, Nan had forgotten about Molly.

The first thing Nan always did when Jasper visited was make a snack. Afterward, they went to the living room to play Go Fish for jujubes. If Jasper won at Go Fish, which he almost always did, he got to take a jujube from the crystal bowl on the coffee table. He always picked a colored one. But if Jasper let Nan win, which he sometimes did, Nan took a black jujube. When all the jujubes were gone, they stopped playing cards.

The crystal bowl was filled to the top. There were twelve red, green, orange and yellow jujubes and four black jujubes. Jasper won twelve games and Nan won four. Then the crystal bowl was empty.

Jasper said, "Okay. Now I'm going to read to you, Nan."

Nan kept the kids' books on the shelf in the spare room. Some were Dad's old books and some were new ones that she'd bought for Jasper. Jasper grabbed one without looking at it and raced back to the living room. He sat on the sofa next to Nan and put the crystal bowl between them.

"What's that for, Jasper?" Nan asked.

"It's the tip jar," Jasper said.

He opened the book. It was an old one of Dad's — so old and so so easy to read. "This is Rover," Jasper read. "Rover is a dog. See Rover sit. See Rover run."

Jasper thought of Molly and her frown. Even though this book was about a dog, she'd be bored by it. He glanced at Nan. Her eyes were closed and she was smiling. Nan was enjoying sitting beside Jasper and listening to the sound of his voice.

"See the ball. See Rover fetch the ball. Good boy, Rover."

Jasper slapped the book shut. "The end!"

Nan opened her eyes. "That was excellent reading, Jasper. Thank you so much."

"Did I do a good job?" Jasper asked.

"Yes, indeed," Nan said.

Jasper smiled at Nan, showing all his teeth. Then

he smiled at the empty crystal bowl between them. When Nan still didn't get the hint, he lifted the crystal bowl and tapped it with his finger the way Ms. Tosh tapped on Jasper's desk whenever he lost focus.

Ping! went the bowl.

"Oh, your tip!" Nan said. "I'm sorry, Jasper."

"I wasn't asking for it," Jasper said. "You're not allowed to ask. You can only hope."

"I'll go get it, Jasper."

Nan pushed herself off the sofa with a grunt and left the room. Jasper heard her rustling around in the kitchen. Then she came back with Jasper's tip.

"Here you go," she said, pouring more jujubes out of the package into the bowl. "You can eat them all. You don't even have to beat me at cards."

Chapter 7

After supper, Dad picked up Jasper from Nan's and drove him home. When they came out of the garage, Jasper saw the garbage bin and remembered that the book they'd killed was inside it.

Jasper thought of something. The book was in a plastic grocery bag. If Mom took out the garbage, she might notice the bag already there holding something rectangular, like a book. She might open the bag and see the dead book. If she did, she'd make Jasper take it back to the library right away.

Then the librarians would know Jasper was a Book Killer and make him pay.

Jasper had to put the book in somebody else's garbage bin.

"I'm just going over to Ori's house for a second," he told Dad. "I'll be right back."

It was still light out so Dad said okay.

Jasper waited until Dad went inside the house. Then he opened the lid of the garbage bin. He yucked because it stank. It stank of garbage and dead book. Jasper pulled out the bag.

He slipped through the back gate and looked up and down the alley. The coast was clear. Right there, across the alley and one house down, stood Ori's garbage bin.

Jasper sprinted over. Ori's garbage bin stank of

diapers. Yuck! Jasper was just about to drop the book in when he thought of something else. Ori's mom might take out their garbage and notice the rectangular shape of the bag already in the bin. She

 might be curious and open it. When she saw the dead book, she might think Ori had killed it.

Jasper hurried farther down the alley, all the way until he reached the last garbage bin. That bin belonged to people they didn't know. He opened it and, gagging, dropped the book in.

"Jasper!" Mom called.

Jasper ran back home. Before Mom could ask what he'd been doing, he asked her, "Did the mail come?"

"It's in the kitchen. Why?"

Jasper was already halfway there.

He leafed through what was lying on the table — a flyer about lawn care and a flyer advertising houses for sale, a coupon book and a reminder card from the dentist. At the bottom of the pile was the phone bill. There wasn't any bill from the library asking Jasper J. Dooley to pay twenty-five and two zeros dollars for the book.

He went to his room and lay on the bed. Mom came in a minute later. "You look tired, Jasper."

"I'm thinking," Jasper said. Ori had to be wrong

about what the book cost. "What's a twenty-five and two zeros?"

"You're thinking about math?" Mom sat beside him and put her hand on his forehead. "Should I call 9-1-1?"

Jasper didn't laugh.

"It's two thousand five hundred."

Jasper sat up with a gasp. "Dollars?"

"If you're counting dollars. Or two thousand five hundred apples. Or two thousand five hundred oranges."

Jasper fell back on the bed again. "I feel sick," he said, hugging his stomach, and not because of apples or oranges.

"Ah, math-itis," Mom said. "Get ready for bed. Then we'll read."

"Read?" Jasper popped right up again. "Okay!"

After he'd put on his pajamas and brushed his teeth, he took his piggy bank off the shelf. He shook it, but the pig didn't jangle. The pig was empty. Whatever money Jasper had had, he'd spent it. But now he had to save.

He fed the tip from Mandy through the slot in the pig's back. The used tickets he crumpled and tossed on the floor. Then he set the empty tip jar on the bedside table and called to Mom.

She came and sat beside him. The book in his lap was called *100 Party Ideas*. Mom said, "This isn't really a bedtime book."

"I picked it for Molly," Jasper told her. "Nobody frowns at a party. What should I read? Circus Party? Mexican Fiesta? Halloween Hoopla?"

Mom said, "You choose."

Jasper read the chapter about the circus party. The best place to have a circus party was in your backyard, or in a gym. He read to Mom about the activity stations — tightrope walking and juggling and pin-the-tail-on-the-lion. He read about the circus snacks and decorations.

After he finished reading, Mom said, "Actually, that was a great book to read together, Jasper. Now I've got some good ideas for your next party."

"How was my reading?" Jasper asked.

"Good," Mom told him. "You're a great reader."

"So I did a good job?" Jasper hinted.

"You read very well." Mom kissed him good night.

"Mom?" Jasper said. He turned his head and looked hopefully at the empty tip jar on the bedside table. When she didn't seem to get the hint, he reached out and tapped it.

Ping! went the jar.

"In this?" Mom asked and Jasper nodded. She picked up the jar and left with it.

A minute later she brought it back and set it on the bedside table again. Jasper made his Book Killer face.

"What's wrong?" Mom asked. "You wanted a glass of water, didn't you?"

Chapter 8

Jasper had a bad dream that night. He dreamed he'd found the money to pay the library, but he couldn't remember where he'd put it. He looked everywhere — under his bed, in his lint box, in all his drawers. Then he smelled something. Something was burning! He rushed to the kitchen and looked in the oven window, at the hungry flames and the twenty-five and two zeros dollars going up in smoke.

In the dream, Jasper screamed.

At lunch the next day, he and Ori headed for the

back of the schoolyard where the playground monitor couldn't see them. They passed Isabel and Margo and Zoë and Bernadette on the way. They were stuffing each other's socks with pinecones again.

"What's the point of that game?" Ori asked Jasper.

"I don't know, but I think it has something to do with that squirrel book."

"Let's get out of here before they start stuffing *our* socks," Ori said.

They sneaked past the girls. Behind the bushes, Jasper flopped down on the ground. He asked Ori to cover him with branches and leave him there when the bell rang.

"Why?" Ori asked.

"I owe two thousand five hundred dollars for a library book. I'll never be able to pay it back."

"That's a lot of money for a book," Ori said.

"I think so, too!" Jasper groaned. He reached for a branch, ripped it off the bush and laid it over his face. "But it was a so so good book. It was about things you can make with toilet-paper tubes."

"You lost it?" Ori asked.

"I disposed of it."

"What does that mean?"

"I got rid of it. So nobody would ever find out what happened to it."

"What happened to it?" Ori asked.

Jasper lifted the branch off his face so Ori could see he'd made a tight line with his mouth.

Ori remembered something then. He leaned right over so that Jasper could smell his breath. It smelled like butterscotch pudding from his lunch. "What

you told me yesterday?" Ori whispered. "About
taking care of my library book? Did something bad
happen to your book?"

Jasper squeezed his eyes shut so he wouldn't see
the black, soggy book with the so so ugly white crust
sticking to it. But closing his eyes made him see it
better. He opened them again.

Ori asked, "Did you drown the book, Jasper?"

"Yes," Jasper blurted.

"And then you set it on fire?"

"No. My dad did."

"So who shot it?" Ori asked.

"The fire extinguisher."

"Can you tell me where you disposed of the book?"

"It's in a garbage can at the end of the alley."

"We have to go and look at it," Ori said.

Jasper propped himself up and stared at Ori. "Are you sure? It's so so so so horrible!"

Mom was on time today. She hardly ever got the lates because she worked at home. Ori asked if Jasper could come over to his house for a playdate.

"I was going to suggest you come to our house,

Ori," Mom said as they walked. "To set up your Read-to-Your-Pet stand again."

"We don't want to," Jasper said. "Hardly any pets came. It was boring."

"I wasn't bored," Ori said. "But today we're doing something else."

They stopped at the alley where Jasper and Ori would turn to go to Ori's house. "Hmm," Mom said. "Now I'm curious. What are you doing?"

The boys made tight lines with their lips. Mom laughed and said, "Oh, go ahead, then."

Ori and Jasper walked normally to Ori's gate. They turned and waved to Mom, who was waiting at the end of the alley to make sure they got to Ori's house safely. Then they closed the gate behind them and crouched down in Ori's yard.

After a minute, they opened the gate and peeked out. The coast was clear. Mom was gone.

"Follow me," Jasper told Ori.

Jasper took off with Ori trotting behind him. Right away, he started to worry that people might see them and wonder what they were up to in the alley, poking around in the garbage bins. He stopped and pressed himself flat against a fence so he wouldn't attract attention. Ori did, too.

They ran a little farther, then pressed against another fence.

"Why do we keep stopping?" Ori asked.

"It's that one," Jasper said, pointing to the bin.

Ori went and flipped open the lid. When they peeked inside, a so so terrible reek rose up. They staggered back, yucking.

Jasper took a deep breath and tried again. A new bag of stinky garbage covered the book.

"We need a stick," he said.

They found a long one lying on the ground nearby. Jasper wriggled the end of the stick into the knot of the garbage bag. Together he and Ori lifted it out and placed it on the ground.

Now when he looked inside the bin, Jasper saw the flat shape of the book. The boys fished it out the same way, by the knot in the bag, and dropped it on the ground. They used the stick to lift the stinky garbage back into the bin.

When they had pulled the book away from the bin, Jasper bent over the bag.

Ori asked, "Why are you making that face?"

Jasper said, "Because I'm a Book Killer."

"Just open it," Ori said.

Jasper grabbed the bag and ripped it open with the stick. They stared down at the burned mess that used to be a book about toilet-paper-tube crafts. Ori cringed. His nose wrinkled. He looked like a Book Killer, too.

"What's that white stuff?" he asked.

"It's from getting extinguished," Jasper said.

Ori crouched and pulled back the plastic so he could see the corner of the book where the price was printed. He took the stick from Jasper and scraped away some of the burned stuff.

"That's what I thought," Ori said. "Do you see it, Jasper?"

He pointed with the stick. Jasper squinted.

"Here," Ori said. "See the two and the five? See the zeros? See what's in between them?"

"Burned stuff," Jasper said.

"Burned stuff and a tiny dot."

Jasper saw it then. A tiny dot between the numbers.

"The thing is, Jasper? That dot just saved your life."

Chapter 9

On Saturday morning, Dad took Jasper to soccer. After the game, they stopped at the concession stand.

"Your coffee costs two dollars and fifty cents," Jasper said, pointing to the board where the prices were written. "My hot dog costs four dollars."

"That's right, Jasper," Dad said. He took a ten-dollar bill from his wallet and handed it to the server with purple streaks in her hair.

"But do you see the dots in the prices?" Jasper asked. "If those dots weren't there, you'd have to pay two hundred and fifty dollars for that coffee and four hundred dollars for the hot dog. I bet you don't have that much money in your wallet."

"You're right," Dad said.

The purple-streaked server gave Dad his change. He dropped the coins in the plastic cup with the word *Tips* written on it. The tip cup was almost full to the top. "You must do a good job," Jasper told the server.

"I hope I do." She smiled and handed Dad his coffee.

"Do you get to keep all that money?" Jasper asked her.

"Yes, but it's not that much when it's dimes and quarters. Here you go." She nestled his hot dog in the bun and passed it to him. "Tell me if it tastes like a four-hundred-dollar hot dog."

Jasper took a bite. "Mmm."

He and Dad went to sit on a bench. While Jasper
ate his hot dog and Dad drank his coffee, they
watched the next group of kids playing soccer.
Between bites, Jasper asked Dad, "How much did
you tip her?"

"I'm not sure. Fifty cents, I think."

Jasper nodded. Just as he thought. "Not very much."

He wasn't ever going to earn enough in tips to pay for the book, even if it was only twenty-five dollars and not two thousand five hundred dollars. Ori had said the same thing yesterday. He'd said, "We have to think of some other way to earn money."

While Jasper ate his hot dog, he waited for some ideas. If he waited long enough, one or two usually came along. He finished eating and wiped his ketchupy fingers on the napkin. They watched the game a little longer.

No ideas came.

"I'll throw this out," Jasper said, taking Dad's empty cup and stuffing his napkin in it. He headed for the garbage bin at the corner of the field, walking backward because it was slower and would give the ideas more time. All the way to the garbage bin and back to the bench, backward.

"I'm glad you didn't play soccer backward," Dad told him.

They both walked forward to the parking lot.

Still no ideas.

As they passed the concession stand, Jasper waved to the purple-streaked server, and she waved back. And suddenly Jasper got a so so good idea!

Jasper explained his idea to Dad as they were driving away. Dad liked it.

"A concession stand?" Mom said when they got home and told her about it. "In our front yard? After school?"

"Yes," Jasper said.

"He wants to earn some money," Dad said.

Mom said, "I have a lot of work this week. I won't be able to help you after school."

"Ori and I will do it ourselves," Jasper told her. "We want to. Then we'll get to keep all the money."

Jasper ran across the alley and one house down to tell Ori his idea. At Ori's house, Ori's baby sister was wa-wa-waing. They called her the Watermelon because that was what she looked like before she was born, like a watermelon stuffed under Ori's mom's shirt. Today, Ori's mom was carrying her around on her hip. With her other hand she was heating up the mushy food that the Watermelon liked.

Jasper explained his concession stand idea to Ori's mom.

"Sounds great," she said. "But don't ask me to cook anything. As you can see, I have my hands full already."

"We're doing everything," Jasper said.

"The thing is," Ori said to Jasper, "we don't know how to cook."

"There must be something we can cook," Jasper said.

"Cheese cubes?" Ori said.

Ori's mom said, "No knives."

But there was a food Jasper was good at cooking! He remembered it when Ori's mom took the Watermelon's mush out of the microwave.

On the counter, sitting next to the microwave, was the toaster.

On Sunday, Ori suggested they make menus.

"A concession stand shows its prices on a sign," Jasper told Ori.

"Do you want to make money?" Ori asked.

"Yes. Twenty-five dollars."

"The food at a concession stand is cheap," Ori said. "If you want to make money, you need a restaurant."

"You mean with plates?" Jasper said.

"And menus. We went to this restaurant once. It was so expensive! My dad said just the tip was more than he paid for a whole dinner in most restaurants. The more the food costs, the more you have to tip."

"Really?" Jasper said. "That's crazy."

"I know. We never went back."

They spent the rest of the afternoon making menus.

"Some people are Raspberry Jam People," Jasper said. "Some people are Strawberry Jam People. And some people are Blueberry Jam People."

the ToAST ResteranT
Fine Dining!

Toast with Butter $1.00
Toast with Butter and Jam $1.50
JAmS you can pick
Strawberry
Blueberry
Rasberry
(more than one kind of jam is 50¢ extra)
We hope you enjoy your toast!
Come to the Toast Resterant!

"But what about the Marmalade People?" Ori asked.

"See what's in your fridge," Jasper said. "Bring it over tomorrow."

Chapter 10

At school on Monday, Jasper and Ori told the class about the Toast Restaurant. They invited all their friends to come by after school.

"A toast restaurant!" Isabel said. "I love toast!"

Zoë said, "But our Cheeky Club is after school, remember?"

"Oh, yeah. Sorry," Isabel said. "Not today."

The girls went back to stuffing their socks with pinecones.

After Mom picked up Jasper and Ori from

school, she offered to make them a snack before they started work.

"The thing is, we're opening our restaurant," Ori said. "We'll make you a snack."

Mom laughed. "Okay. I'll drop by when I get hungry."

Jasper and Ori carried out the things they needed: Jasper's small table and two small chairs, a cardboard box that they turned on its side to be a counter and a cupboard for the bread, butter and jam. They brought out plates and the empty jar for tips. They found a so so so long extension cord that reached all the way inside the house. Then they plugged in the toaster. Ori taped the Toast Restaurant Fine Dining sign to the tree.

They waited.

"I hope Rollo doesn't come," Ori said. "He'll eat all the toast."

"Except that Mandy would pay us," Jasper said.

"You're right. I hope Rollo comes!"

They waited some more. Mom looked out the window and waved. Jasper waved back.

Ori said he was hungry. Jasper handed him a menu. Ori studied it for a minute, then said, "I think I'll have toast."

"That's a good choice," Jasper said. He went behind the counter, took a slice of bread from the bag and put it in the toaster. "Light or dark?"

"I can choose?" Ori asked.

"That's what this knob is for." Jasper showed him how to adjust the toast color.

"You really do know how to cook toast, Jasper!" Ori chose light.

Jasper turned the knob. A few minutes later, when the toast popped up, it was a perfect light brown.

"Butter?" Jasper asked. "It's included in the price."

Ori nodded.

"And what kind of jam? Strawberry, blueberry or raspberry? Or you can have all three."

"All three!" Ori said.

"Mixed or in stripes?" Jasper asked. "Stripes keep the flavors separate."

Ori picked stripes. Jasper jammed the toast with the three jams, put it on a plate and carried it over to Ori sitting at the table.

"That's one dollar and fifty cents plus fifty cents plus fifty cents."

"What?" Ori said.

"Fifty cents extra for each different kind of jam. Remember?"

Ori frowned. "You're not really going to make me pay, are you? I'm helping you."

"You can owe me," Jasper said. "Look! A customer!"

It was Ori's mom coming along with the Watermelon in the stroller.

"Oh, good," she said as she got closer. "I was just starting to feel hungry. May I see your menu?"

Jasper handed it to her. Ori's mom ordered toast with butter.

"And what about the Watermelon?" Jasper asked.

"She'll share with me."

Ori's mom asked Ori if he minded sitting at the same table with her.

"You can if you pay for my toast," Ori told her.

Mom looked out the window again. When she saw Ori's mom, she came out of the house and joined her for a piece of toast. There weren't any more chairs so she sat on the grass. She was a Strawberry Jam Person.

While the two mothers were eating and chatting, and the Watermelon was sucking on her crust, Jasper walked back and forth in front of them with the tip jar. He drummed his fingernails against it.

Ping! Ping! Ping! Ping! Ping!

The mothers didn't notice. The Watermelon laughed.

Ori's mom finished her toast. "I just realized, Jasper, that I don't have my wallet with me. I'll pay you later. Ori, time to come home."

"Already?" Jasper said.

Ori stood to go. "Bye, Jasper," he said. "I hope you make some money. You need it."

Jasper frowned good-bye.

After they left, Jasper told Mom, "Now I have to close the restaurant!"

"But it was fun, wasn't it?" Mom said. "I'll help you put everything away."

She picked up the table and carried it inside. Jasper started to load the cardboard box, but he had to stop because he was mad. So so so mad! Mad tears were pricking at his eyes.

"It wasn't fun!" he told Mom when she came back out. "Nobody paid me anything! Do you think people leave a real fine dining restaurant without paying? And nobody gave me a tip!"

"You'll get your money, Jasper," Mom said.

"How long till Wednesday?" Jasper asked.

"Two days."

"I have two days to find twenty-five dollars!" Jasper shouted.

"Why do you need so much money? And why by Wednesday?" Mom asked.

"Because that's the next time Molly is at the library! Nan wants to go with me!"

A loud rumble interrupted his shouting. He turned and saw the nose of the garbage truck poking out of the alley into the street. Then the truck turned and rattled right past them, trailing a horrible stink. It was the stink of the dead library book.

Jasper burst into tears.

He was crying because he had killed that book. He'd killed the book and still owed twenty-five dollars to the library for it. Then he was crying because he'd probably never get a turn to read to Molly. He only calmed down when Mom popped a piece of bread into the toaster that was sitting on the lawn attached to the so so so long extention cord. She jammed the toast with stripes — raspberry, blueberry and strawberry — and handed it to him.

"Thank you!" Jasper wailed.

When Dad got home from work, Mom was waiting with crossed arms. Jasper was still puffy from crying.

Dad looked from Mom to Jasper. "What happened?"

Jasper burst out, "I told her about the book!"

At first Dad didn't seem to know what book Jasper was talking about. Then he remembered.

"Oh, that book." To Mom he said, "We had a little accident with the book, Gail. When the bill comes, I'll take care of it."

Mom said, "But David, poor Jasper thought that he had to pay twenty-five dollars to the library before he'd be allowed back. He even had a bad dream about it."

"I'm sorry, Jasper," Dad said. "I didn't realize you were upset."

They decided to talk about it over supper, so Jasper went to set the table. The library book that was still alive, *100 Party Ideas*, was lying there with the mail.

"No bill yet," Jasper told Dad as he collected the pile of flyers.

After they sat down to eat, Dad told Jasper, "I'll give you the money to take to the library the next time you go. I would have done that earlier if you'd asked me."

"You shouldn't have to pay for the whole book," Jasper said. "I'm the one who drowned it."

"You drowned it," Dad said, "but I set it on fire."

"And shot it," Jasper said.

"Oh," Mom said, laying down her fork. "The things that happen around here when I'm not home!"

"Since you only drowned it, but I shot it and set it on fire," Dad said, "you pay one-third and I'll pay two-thirds."

"Except I told you to shoot it," Jasper said.

"Okay," Dad said. "We'll go halvesies then."

"This is math, isn't it?" Jasper said. "How much do I have to pay?"

"I'm paying twelve dollars and fifty cents," Dad said.

Then Jasper laid down his fork, too. "How am I going to get twelve dollars and fifty cents by Wednesday?"

"I'm sure you'll think of something," Mom said. "You always do."

"Hmm," Jasper said.

This time the idea came fast. All Jasper had to do was glance at the counter where he had stacked the library book and the flyers.

Chapter 11

On Wednesday they didn't go to the library. Instead of waiting for Jasper and Ori at the front of the school, Mom met them in the classroom. She brought their flyer to show Ms. Tosh. They wanted her permission to tell the class about their plan.

Ms. Tosh said, "Are you telling me that these two boys who are always whispering and laughing in the Book Nook are actually putting on a reading party?"

"It's a Read to Your Pet Fiesta Party Hoopla Celebration," Ori said.

"With toast!" Jasper said.

Ms. Tosh studied the flyer. "I see you'll have stations for Dogs, Cats, Hamsters, Bears, Spiders and Other Pets. Are you sure about Bears? Won't that be Very Dangerous?"

"Teddy Bears," Ori told her.

Ms. Tosh's favorite was the Read to a Spider Station.

"It's a toilet-paper-tube spider," Jasper told her. "Or you can bring your own spider."

"Something special is going to happen at the end," Ori said.

"So you're putting on this party to pay back the library?" Ms. Tosh asked.

"That's right," Jasper said. "I owe them twelve dollars and fifty cents. But twenty-five dollars would be better."

"So the more people who come, the more you'll make?"

Jasper nodded.

"Then why not have a Squirrel Station? Everybody's crazy about those Cheeky books."

Jasper stared at Ms. Tosh for a second. Then he clapped his hand across his forehead.

"Ms. Tosh, you astound me. We didn't think of that."

The day before the Read to Your Pet Fiesta Party Hoopla Celebration, while Jasper and Ori and Ori's dad walked around the neighborhood pushing the Watermelon in the stroller and delivering flyers, Jasper counted seven clouds in the sky. Ori said not to worry. They were the white, cotton-bally kind of clouds, not the gray, rainy kind of clouds.

The morning of the Fiesta Party Hoopla Celebration there were more clouds. They didn't look like cotton balls.

"What if it rains?" Jasper said over his toast at breakfast.

"I don't think it's going to," Dad said.

"But if it does? The pages of all the books will stick together, and the toast will get soggy. And nobody will come to our Fiesta Party Hoopla Celebration."

"It won't rain," Dad said.

After breakfast, Ori came over with the special thing that was going to end the Fiesta Party Hoopla Celebration — the rocket he'd made out of a soda bottle. They set up the signs for the stations. Under each sign they spread a blanket and left a pile of books. At the Read to Your Bear Station they also put a teddy for the people who forgot to bring bears.

At the Read to Your Spider Station, they put the toilet-paper-tube spider that Jasper had made, for the people who didn't have their own spiders. They didn't have a toy squirrel. Mom found a picture in a calendar to tape to a tree.

"I think we should put the Squirrel Station in the front yard. It's getting crowded back here," she said. Then she saw Ori's rocket. "Ori, what is that? It looks dangerous!"

"My dad's going to help me fire it," he promised.

Dad plugged in the extension cord and set up the Toast Station. Jasper brought out a shoebox with a slot he'd cut in the lid for collecting the money.

Mom got to work tying streamers to the fence. When she was nearly finished, Jasper came to ask the time.

"You tell me." Mom showed him her watch.

Ugh! Hands! "Is it one o'clock yet?"

Dad checked his watch. "I'd better go pick up Nan."

As soon as Nan arrived and took her place at the ticket table, some of the girls from Jasper's class showed up wearing pink ballet outfits and tights with lumps. They started twirling and cartwheeling and waving their Cheeky books around.

Mom rushed over.

"Isabel? Margo? Zoë? The Squirrel Station is right here." She pointed to the blanket under the squirrel picture taped to the tree.

The girls chanted, "Cheeky! Cheeky! Cheeky!" and twirled some more.

People began lining up with their pets. They dropped their money in the slot in the lid of the shoebox and took their ticket. Everybody but the squirrel readers headed to the backyard. Rollo came with Mandy and a white dog Jasper had never seen before. The yellow Lab from across the street came with her owner. A Grade Four girl brought two gerbils in a cage. Someone brought a cat, but when it saw the dogs, it squirmed out of its owner's arms and ran away.

Paul C. brought Hammy the Hamster from school. It was his turn to look after Hammy for the weekend. Patty brought her caterpillar in a jar. There was even a woman they didn't know with a parrot on her shoulder.

"Thank you very much!" the parrot screeched when Nan gave the woman a ticket. "Thank you very much!"

More and more squirrel girls came, and so so many kids with stuffed toys. The sound of stories filled the yard, stories and toast popping and crunching.

"Once upon a time …"

"And they lived happily ever after …"

POP! POP! CRUNCH! CRUNCH!

Ori and Jasper made toast as fast as they could. Ori popped the bread in the toaster. Jasper buttered and jammed. Mom and Ori's dad handed out paper plates of toast to the kids waiting to read to their bears. The dogs licked the crumbs off the grass.

"Look, there's Leon," Ori said. "Leon! What are you doing?"

Leon was crawling around in the shrubs at the back of the yard.

"I'm looking for a spider to read to!" he called.

Then Ms. Tosh dropped by. Jasper and Ori had never seen her outside of school before. "The party sounded like fun," she said.

Jasper was so so careful jamming Ms. Tosh's toast. He jammed so that the stripes didn't overlap. At school, she always encouraged them to color in the lines.

After about an hour of toast making, Jasper looked up and saw even more arrivals — clouds. He started to count them but gave up. There were probably seven and two zeros clouds hanging over them, clouds that didn't look like cotton balls. They looked more like smoke when it pours thick and black from the oven.

"I'm so glad these books aren't from the library," Jasper told Ori. "And I think you should fire the rocket now."

"Already?"

Ori went to get his dad.

"Stand back! Stand back!" they called, and all the readers and their pets and the people waiting to read moved away from the blankets to the edges of the yard.

Ori's dad unscrewed the cap of the soda bottle rocket. Ori opened the package of mints. He looked around at everybody and said, "Watch this!"

At that moment, just as Ori was about to add the mints to the soda bottle and close the cap and shake it, the black clouds hanging over the Read to Your Pet Fiesta Party Hoopla Celebration let go all their rain.

It poured down. "Save the books!" Jasper yelled. People rushed around gathering up the books and hurrying to get them in the house. They snatched up the blankets. Dad unplugged the toaster and ran inside with it. When everything that needed to stay dry was inside, everybody and their pets headed for home before they got completely soaked.

Ori stayed to help Nan and Jasper count the money. They'd sold sixty-seven tickets and earned thirty-three dollars and fifty cents.

"We did it! Hurray!"

Jasper and Ori took off running through the house, hurraying, but when they reached the living room, they stopped. Out the window they saw three girls in the front yard. Three girls wearing lumpy tights, leaping and cartwheeling in the rain.

Isabel, Zoë and Bernadette.

Jasper opened the front door. "Hey, you ballerinas! The party's over!"

"We're not ballerinas!" the girls shouted back. "We're squirrels!"

Mom came to the door and made the girls come in and dry off. Dad brought towels.

"Look at your books," Ori told them. "They're all wet."

"The pages will stick together," Jasper said.

"Don't worry about that," Mom told them. "I know just what to do."

She left and came back with the hairdryer. Jasper looked at Dad and Dad looked at him. Both of them groaned.

Bernadette and Zoë laid their books on the coffee table and took turns with the hairdryer while Ori turned the pages for them. Isabel said her book was fine.

"I'm a squirrel and I want you to read to me," she told Jasper.

She pulled him over to the sofa and thrust the damp Cheeky book in his hands. Jasper tried to stand up again, but she yanked him back down by the arm.

There was no escape. It was just like when the girls made Jasper and Ori play babies at school.

Jasper opened the book. "Glub, glub, glub."

"I paid for my ticket," Isabel said. "You have to read properly."

She was right.

"Chapter One …" he read.

In Chapter One, Cheeky's mother signed her up for ballet. She bought her a tutu and forced Cheeky to wear it even though it was stiff and scratchy and Cheeky hated it. Then Cheeky got a squirrely idea. She decided to use the tutu for her nest. She stuffed it into a hole in a tree.

That was as far as Jasper got before he flopped down laughing.

Chapter 12

After school on Monday, Jasper's mom met the boys and hurried them along.

"The thing is, I'm walking as fast as I can," Ori said. "But my ankles hurt."

"What's wrong with your ankles?" Mom asked.

Ori stopped walking to pull up his pant legs.

"You've got scratches all over them, Ori," Mom said. "What from?"

"Pinecones."

"Where are your socks?"

"In my bag. Full of pinecones."

Jasper explained. "We couldn't find any nuts."

Mom suggested Ori roll his pants so they didn't rub against his scratches. That did the trick. They collected their bikes and helmets from home and rode to the library together — so so so fast — so they could get a good place in line.

At the library, Mom handed Jasper the money in an envelope. "Go ahead and pay while I lock the bikes. I'll bring your books."

Jasper and Ori raced up the steps and pushed open the door. Sitting behind her desk like a hen on a nest was the same nice librarian who had helped them last time. She smiled at Jasper and Ori and pointed to the three kids in line.

Jasper walked straight to her desk and slid his library card across to her.

"I need to pay for a book before I read to Molly."

The librarian bleeped his card. "You have two books checked out. Which one are you paying for?"

"The one about toilet-paper-tube crafts."

Jasper unfolded the envelope of money and gave it to her. "I didn't feel good about using the library when I'd ruined a book."

"Ruined? What happened to it?"

"I'd rather not say." Jasper made a tight line with his lips.

"Oh, don't worry," the librarian said. "I've heard it all. Did you leave it on the roof of the car then drive away so the book fell onto the road and got run over a hundred times?"

"Did someone do that?" Ori asked.

"Yes. Did you use it to start a campfire?"

"What?" Jasper said. "No!"

"Did the dog go wee wee on it?"

"He doesn't have a dog," Ori said.

Jasper leaned in to whisper, "Have you ever heard of somebody doing this — drowning a book in the bathtub, then setting it on fire in the oven, then extinguishing it?"

"Oh, sure. That happens about twice a year," the librarian said. "Now, if you boys want a turn to read to Molly, you'd better get in line."

Jasper and Ori dashed over. Five fidgety kids were waiting to read to Molly, including Jasper and Ori. Jasper looked around for Mom. Three more kids got in line behind him. Jasper moved up one place. Then

Mom came in the door and handed Jasper and Ori their Cheeky books from school.

Jasper stepped to the front. His turn was next, after a boy with red hair. There was Molly, in his lap, still looking grumpy.

"The end," read the boy.

Molly's owner lifted Molly out of his lap. She smiled at Jasper.

Finally, it was his turn! He plopped down in the big, comfy chair. It was warm from the other kids who had read to Molly before Jasper. Molly's owner settled Molly into his lap.

"Don't worry, Molly," Jasper told her. "You're going to love this book."

Molly lifted her funny pushed-in face and stared at Jasper with her huge brown eyes.

Jasper read Chapter Six, where on the night of the
ballet performance, Cheeky arrived tutuless, with
her nuts stored in her tights.

Molly the Dog, warm in his lap, started bouncing up and down with Jasper as he laughed. Mom was standing beside Molly's owner, listening to him read and enjoying the sound of his voice. She was laughing, too. So were Ori and Molly's owner. And Molly's tail was wagging!

Molly's owner only stopped laughing to say, "That's five minutes."

"Already?" Jasper said.

When Molly's owner lifted Molly out of Jasper's lap, cool air filled the warm place where she'd been. Jasper's turn was already over after he'd waited so so long for the chance. He'd just reached the best part, where Cheeky tries to dance gracefully with all those nuts in her tights. He would have felt sad, except he couldn't. He was laughing too hard.

Praise for
the Jasper John Dooley series

Jasper John Dooley: Star of the Week

★ Best Children's Books of the Year, Bank Street Children's Book Committee

"Well-written, funny, and engaging ... Share with kids looking for a boy version of Sara Pennypacker's Clementine series or with fans of Lenore Look's Alvin Ho books." — *Booklist*

Jasper John Dooley: Left Behind

★ Named to *Kirkus Reviews'* Best Books of 2013

★ "So aptly, charmingly and amusingly depicted that it's impossible not to be both captivated and compelled." — *Kirkus Reviews,* starred review

Jasper John Dooley: NOT in Love

★ Named to *Kirkus Reviews'* Best Books of 2014

★ "Adderson perfectly captures the trials of early childhood, and with brief text and a simple vocabulary, she breathes full life into her cast of characters." — *Kirkus Reviews,* starred review

Jasper John Dooley: You're in Trouble

★ "Another highly entertaining and enthusiastic outing in a series that's perfect for readers new to chapter books and as a captivating read-aloud." — *Kirkus Reviews,* starred review